JACK
AND THE
BEANSTALK

Retold by Rita Balducci
Illustrated by Richard Walz

A GOLDEN BOOK • NEW YORK
Golden Books Publishing Company, Inc., Racine, Wisconsin 53404

Once upon a time there was a young boy named Jack. He lived with his mother in a simple cottage. They were poor and had barely enough to eat. Their only possession in the world was a cow.

One day Jack's mother said to him, "We have no money left to buy food. We will have to sell our cow. Take her into town and get the best price you can."

And so Jack led the cow down the road toward town. He hadn't gone far when he met a strange little man. "What an excellent beast!" cried the man, patting Jack's cow. "I must have her for my own."

"What will you give me in return?" asked Jack.

"Why, I'll trade you these beans for the cow," said the little man. "They're magic."

Jack's eyes grew wide. "It's a deal," he said happily.

The little man handed Jack some shiny red beans. Then he quickly disappeared with the cow.

Jack was very excited. He ran home as fast as he could.
"Mother, I traded the cow for some magic beans!"

"Oh, Jack!" his mother cried. "How could you? Now our
cow is gone, and all we have are these hard little beans.
You've been tricked!"

She was so upset that she threw the beans out the window into the dry, empty garden.

There was no supper that night for Jack and his mother. They went to bed with hearts heavy with worry.

When Jack awoke the next morning, his room was dark and cool. "It must be a cloudy day," he thought, poking his head out the window.

Jack gasped. It was not clouds that were blocking the sun. It was a tremendous beanstalk growing in the garden. Its leaves were as wide as a bed. Its trunk was as big as the cottage. Jack stretched his neck to see how high it grew, but the top of the stalk disappeared into the clouds.

   Quick as a wink, Jack scrambled out of the window
and began to climb the beanstalk. High into the soft
white clouds he climbed until he found himself before
a gigantic castle with a huge wooden door.

Jack was able to squeeze through a crack in the wood.
What he saw inside made him shiver with fright. A horrible
giant was seated at a table, slurping an enormous bowl
of soup.

Suddenly the giant stood up and slammed his huge fist on the table. The whole room shook. Dishes crashed to the floor.

"Fee, fi, fo, fum! I smell the blood of a Little One," roared the giant. Then he looked around the room wildly, but he didn't see Jack, who was hiding behind a bucket.

The giant sat down again, grumbling to himself. Jack watched as the giant reached into a sack and pulled out a tiny white hen. He placed the hen on the table.

"Lay me an egg. Add to my treasure. Make me rich
beyond all measure!" the giant commanded. The little
hen clucked and laid a shiny golden egg!

Jack tiptoed closer to look at the gleaming golden egg.
He couldn't believe what he was seeing.

The giant then brought out a beautiful little harp from the cupboard and placed it on the table. "A song for me—and do your best. I need a song to take my rest," the giant said to the harp.

The magical harp began to sing a beautiful, sweet song. Soon the giant was lulled to sleep.

Jack was amazed. "A harp that can sing!" he said to himself. "A hen that lays golden eggs! I must take these treasures home with me." Like a little mouse, Jack scurried across the wide floor and quickly climbed up the table leg.

Then he tucked the hen into his shirt and slipped
the harp under his arm. But the harp began to cry out,
waking the giant.

"Fee, fi, fo, fum!" thundered the giant, rising to his feet.
"Who dares to steal from the Giant One?"

Jack raced out of the castle, with the giant right behind him. The hen clucked and the harp screamed, but Jack never looked back. He began to climb down the beanstalk as fast as he could.

Suddenly the beanstalk shook mightily. The giant was climbing down after Jack. Jack scrambled down even faster. When he neared the ground, he jumped and ran. And just in time, for . . .

CRACK! The beanstalk broke in two. Down, down the giant fell. He crashed into the ground, deep into the earth, and was gone forever.

Jack's mother ran from the cottage when she heard the commotion. "Why, that's your father's hen and harp!" she cried. "A terrible giant stole them from us years ago. Now that we have our treasures back, we'll never go hungry again." And so Jack and his mother lived happily ever after.